SECRET of the MAGIC POTION

Written by Elizabeth Bolton
Illustrated by Blanche Sims

Troll Associates

Library of Congress Cataloging in Publication Data

Bolton, Elizabeth.
    Secret of the magic potion.

    Summary: Betsy's aunt sends her a mysterious potion
that has the power to grant wishes but must be used very
carefully.
    1. Children's stories, American.   [1. Magic—
Fiction.   2. Wishes—Fiction]   I. Sims, Blanche, ill.
II. Title.
PZ7.B63597Sfm   1985   [Fic]   84-8881
ISBN 0-8167-0420-1 (lib. bdg.)
ISBN 0-8167-0421-X (pbk.)

SECRET of the MAGIC POTION

It all started with this box from Aunt
Bedelia. She's my mom's older sister.
She's really weird, but I like her a lot.

Once when I was little, Aunt Bedelia was
baby-sitting. Right before it was time to go to
bed, she said, "I feel like ice cream, Betsy.
How about you?" She dressed me and took
me out for an ice-cream cone. That's the kind
of aunt she is.

When Aunt Bedelia's name comes up, Mom just sighs. Dad calls her "that crazy lady." But *I* think she's great—especially when she sends me presents.

Aunt Bedelia is the kind of person who forgets birthdays. Then she sends a present for the first day of spring. Once she gave me

bright red nail polish and her old high-heeled shoes. Another time she sent me chopsticks after her trip to China. Last time, she sent me perfume from India. It smelled the house up for a week. Dad said either the perfume went or he did. Our cat Toby stayed away till the smell was gone.

This time a present came in the beginning
of October. "BETSY MIDDLETON" the box
was labeled. It had funny foreign words
printed on the wrapper. There was no gift
card. But we knew right away it came from
Aunt Bedelia.

"I wonder what that crazy lady's up to now," Dad said. Mom just sighed. Toby circled the box and sniffed. His tail arched like a question mark.

Inside the box was a purple box. In the purple box was *another* box. That one had orange and yellow stripes. Inside that box

was a big piece of shiny red fabric.

"It's a cape," Mom said. "It must be a costume for Halloween."

I pulled out a shiny red hat. It was tall
and pointed and had gold stars on it.
"It could be a witch's costume," I said.
"But I thought witches wear black."

12

"Maybe not the witches your Aunt
Bedelia knows," said Dad, with a grin.
"Is there anything else in the box, Betsy?"

There were crumpled papers of all different colors. There were torn bits and streamers. Under all the paper was a fat envelope. It was sealed. On it was written: *For Betsy*. PRIVATE!!!

Mom sighed again.

"Now, Lucy," Dad said. Lucy is my
mom's name. "It's Betsy's present. Let her
have her secrets. Bedelia wouldn't give her
something she shouldn't have."

"What about that red nail polish?" Mom
asked.

I was already planning to wear the red
nail polish with the red cape and hat for
Halloween. Maybe there was a really horrible
mask inside the envelope! I took everything
up to my room and shut the door. I pulled

down all the shades, sat on my bed, and
opened the envelope.

A stick fell out. It was dark and smooth.
I reached into the envelope again.

I pulled out a little book. The pages were thin. I could almost see through them. Strange birds and dragons were printed on the cover. The words on the cover sent a shiver down my spine:

HOW TO CAST SPELLS

Maybe Aunt Bedelia did know some real witches! I didn't know whether to be excited or scared. I took a deep breath and opened the book.

The first page said:

How to Make Yourself Invisible
How to Make Writing Disappear
How to Turn Salt to Sugar
How to Make the Sun Shine
How to Make Rain

There were all kinds of great spells. I couldn't wait to try being invisible in science class.

I felt in the envelope again. My fingers found something small. It was wrapped in paper and tied with green cord. The cord

20

was sealed with green sealing wax. I took a
deep breath and broke the seal.

Inside was a small glass bottle. Its cap
was screwed on tight. There was no label.
But the paper it was wrapped in was a note
from Aunt Bedelia.

Dear Betsy,

This is a very special magic potion. I got it just for you. Take good care of it and don't waste it. Wait till you wish for something very, very hard. Then sprinkle the potion. Your wish will come true! Be sure you only wish for *sensible* things! I can't get any more when this is gone.

Love,
Aunt Bedelia

P.S. This is our secret.

I felt that shiver go down my spine again.

I sat for a long time looking at the bottle. I was thinking of all the things I could wish for. The potion was too special to use for most of them. At last, I hid the bottle at the bottom of my dresser drawer.

I told my friends about the cape and hat for Halloween. I told my best friend Kim about the wand and book of spells. I didn't tell *anybody* about the glass bottle.

I wished Aunt Bedelia would come to visit. I wished I knew what she meant by "sensible" wishes.

I did try some of the spells in the book.

I made my arithmetic homework disappear.
That was not a good idea. I tried to make
myself invisible in science class. I don't know
if it worked. The teacher didn't call on me
that day, though.

I didn't try out the magic potion. I almost
forgot about it.

Halloween came and the sun did shine
that day. Maybe that was because of my
spell. Maybe it would have anyway. I wished
I knew!

"I keep waiting for Betsy to make a real
disaster happen," Dad teased when he saw

me in my cape and hat. A real disaster did
happen the next day. But it wasn't my book
of spells that caused it.

Toby went prowling in the woods on
Halloween night. He didn't come home till
morning. And when he did—

"PHEEUWWW!" cried Dad.

"Somebody put a spell on him!" I
shouted.

"Toby had an argument with a skunk,"

Mom said. "Oh, dear! We'll have to buy a lot of tomato juice and give Toby a bath in it. That's supposed to get rid of the skunk smell."

After school, Kim came home with me. We pulled Toby out from under the porch. Mom brought a big bucket and the tomato juice. We held Toby down in the bucket. Mom poured the tomato juice all over him.

Toby did not like it! He kicked and scratched and spit.

"Poor Toby!" Mom said. "Don't worry. This will be over soon." Toby's fluffy gray fur turned red. He looked skinny and soggy and half his size. Then Mom washed him in soap and water. Now his fur clung to him like wet leaves. But he still smelled.

"That settles it!" Mom said. "He'll have to stay outdoors till the smell wears off."

She gave me an old towel to dry him with. Kim went home. She was all wet, too. Mom cleaned up the mess and took the bucket back inside.

Toby and I looked at each other.
"*Mrrowww,*" he said sadly. He looked like
a wet rat. He rubbed against my ankles and
went to the door.

"You can't go in," I told him.

"Mrrowww," Toby said again. He pushed
his head against my foot.

I thought how awful I'd feel if I were
Toby. I thought of the book of spells.
Maybe it told how to take away smells.

It didn't. Then I remembered the little
glass bottle!

This was something I could use it for!
I wanted very much to take away Toby's
skunk smell. That was a sensible wish.

I got the bottle from my bottom drawer. I put it in my pocket. "This is our secret," Aunt Bedelia's letter had said. That was a good reason not to tell Mom what I was doing.

How glad she'll be when the skunk smell's gone, I thought. How glad Toby will be when he can come inside. "What a great magician Betsy Middleton is," everyone will say!

I went back outside. Toby was still wet and sad. I carried him to the river bank in our back yard. Magicians always perform secret spells in private.

While Toby sat on a big rock on the river bank, I unscrewed the top of the bottle. It was hard work. At last a spiral of smoke came out. The potion smelled sweet— like perfume and strange flowers.

"Here goes," I told Toby. I closed my eyes tight and wished hard:

"Wish I may, wish I might,
Take away the skunk smell Toby got last night!"

Spells are always supposed to sound grand and important. I tipped the bottle just a little over Toby's head.

"*Yoww!*" cried Toby.

When I opened my eyes, Toby was staring at me in surprise. I stared, too. The smell was gone, but so was poor Toby's fur! In its place were bright green feathers!

"Oh, no!" I cried.

Toby rubbed against my ankles. He was asking for help. I scrunched my eyes again and wished:

"Wish again and wish some more,
Wish Toby's fur was back,
better than before!"

"Yoww!" cried the cat.

Toby's feathers were gone, and his fur was back. But now he had too much fur. Toby looked like a giant fur hat!

Mom and Dad weren't going to like this.

I had to do something fast. I could hear Mom
calling me.

"*Rrrr,*" said Toby. I'm sure he wished I
hadn't tried to help.

Then I knew what to do.

I closed my eyes tight. I wished as hard as
I could. I didn't even bother sounding grand.
"I wish everything back the way it's supposed

to be! I wish I'd never tried to fix things up by magic. I wish I wasn't a magician!" And I poured the rest of the potion out over Toby.

Again I smelled perfume and strange flowers. The empty glass bottle twisted in my hands. It fell into the river and floated away.

Something pushed against my ankle. It was Toby's head. I opened my eyes. Toby was wet and skinny. His fur was soggy and smelled of skunk. Everything was just the way it was before!

Then I knew what Aunt Bedelia meant.
You have to be careful when you wish for
things. You may get what you want. But you
may not want what you get.

I'll know better next time I wish for
things, just as Toby will know better than to
argue with a skunk. Toby and I ran home.

Everything turned out all right. Toby's skunk smell soon wore off. My book of spells and cape and hat had mysteriously disappeared. And that was the end of my brief career as a magician.

I was happy to have everything back to normal. But sometimes I still wish I could become invisible in science class!